Documents That Shaped America

The
UNITED STATES
CONSTITUTION

By Therese Shea

Gareth Stevens
Publishing

Please visit our website, www.garethstevens.com. For a free color catalog of all our high-quality books, call toll free 1-800-542-2595 or fax 1-877-542-2596.

Library of Congress Cataloging-in-Publication Data

Shea, Therese.
The United States Constitution / by Therese Shea.
  p. cm. — (Documents that shaped America)
Includes index.
ISBN 978-1-4339-9010-6 (pbk.)
ISBN 978-1-4339-9011-3 (6-pack)
ISBN 978-1-4339-9009-0 (library binding)
1. Constitutional law — United States — Juvenile literature. 2. Constitutional history — United States — Juvenile literature. I. Shea, Therese. II. Title.
KF4550.Z9 S43 2014
342.73—d23

First Edition

Published in 2014 by
Gareth Stevens Publishing
111 East 14th Street, Suite 349
New York, NY 10003

Copyright © 2014 Gareth Stevens Publishing

Designer: Sarah Liddell
Editor: Therese Shea

Photo credits: Cover, p. 1 photo courtesy of Wikimedia Commons, Scene at the Signing of the Constitution of the United States.jpg; p. 4 photo courtesy of Wikimedia Commons, Articles page1.jpg; p. 5 Antar Dayal/Illustration Works/Getty Images; p. 6 Hulton Archive/Stringer/Hulton Archive/Getty Images; p. 7 After Augustus Kollner/ The Bridgeman Art Library/Getty Images; p. 9 DEA PICTURE LIBRARY/Contributor/ De Agostini/Getty Images; p. 10 DEA/M. SEEMULLER/Contributor/De Agostini/ Getty Images; pp. 11, 19 Stock Montage/Contributor/Archive Photos/Getty Images; p. 13 (Federalist papers) photo courtesy of Wikimedia Commons, Federalist Papers.jpg; p. 13 (Hamilton) Kean Collection/Staff/Archive Photos/Getty Images; p. 13 (John Jay) DEA PICTURE LIBRARY/De Agostini Picture Library/Getty Images; p. 13 (Madison) Popperfoto/Contributor/Popperfoto/Getty Images; p. 15 (Gouverneur Morris) Hulton Archive/Stringer/Archive Photos/Getty Images; p. 15 (Preamble) Steve McAlister/Photographer's Choice/Getty Images; p. 17 photo courtesy of Wikimedia Commons, Constitution of the Unites States, page 1.jpg; p. 20 Dwight Nadig/E+/ Getty Images; p. 21 Encyclopaedia Britannica/Contributor/Universal Images Group/ Getty Images; p. 23 photo courtesy of Wikimedia Commons, 13th Amendment Pg1of1 AC.jpg; p. 25 Photri Images/SuperStock/Getty Images; p. 27 Chip Somodevilla/Staff/ Getty Images News/Getty Images; p. 28 photo courtesy of Wikimedia Commons, Constitution of India.jpg.

Printed in the United States of America

CPSIA compliance information: Batch #CS13GS: For further information contact Gareth Stevens, New York, New York at 1-800-542-2595.

CONTENTS

Words in the glossary appear in **bold** type the first time they are used in the text.

The FIRST CONSTITUTION

Not everyone knows there was a US **constitution** before our current one. It was called the Articles of Confederation. A confederation is a group of states that acts together for some purposes but allows each state to keep its independence.

This independence that the original states held dear was part of the reason why the Articles of Confederation was an ineffective constitution. Under the Articles, there was no executive branch, or president. There was no national court system. Though there was a Congress, at least nine of the 13 states needed to agree with its decisions before many laws could go into effect. Congress could declare war, but it couldn't raise an army without the consent and **militias** of the states. The newly created United States was weak and open to attack.

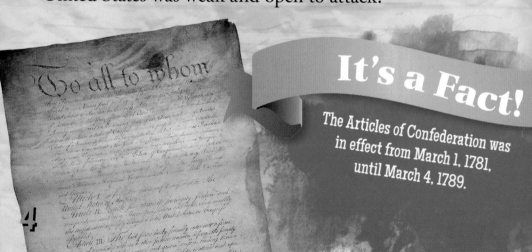

It's a Fact!

The Articles of Confederation was in effect from March 1, 1781, until March 4, 1789.

4

A draft of the Articles of Confederation handwritten by Benjamin Franklin can be found in the National Archives in Washington, DC.

NOT A NATION, A CONFEDERATION

After the American Revolution, many of the Founding Fathers were worried about creating a central government that was too strong. Americans had suffered under the powerful British government. They feared a similar authority would step on people's rights one day. It seemed safer to let each state rule itself. There isn't even mention of a "country" or "nation" in the Articles of Confederation. Instead, the **document** stresses that each state would keep its powers and freedoms.

Taxation without representation was one of the issues behind the American Revolution. It was still on the minds of the representatives who created the Articles of Confederation. The Congress of the Confederation had no power to collect taxes. Only the states could impose taxes. If individual states didn't want to help pay for the national government, they simply didn't have to. Therefore, the debts from the war were left unpaid—including salaries of soldiers who had fought for the freedom of the nation!

The situation was so bad that in 1783 former soldiers threatened to take Congress hostage until they were paid. Congress, then in Philadelphia, asked Pennsylvania to send militia to help them. Pennsylvania refused. Truly, the so-called "United" States had a hard time being united in most matters.

It's a Fact!

During Shays' **Rebellion** of 1786 and 1787, farmers in great debt protested against the Massachusetts state government. Other states feared similar uprisings.

The Congress of the Confederation had to move from the state house in Philadelphia, shown here, because of the soldiers' threats. They had meetings in Princeton, New Jersey; Annapolis, Maryland; and New York City.

PIRATES AND OTHER THREATS

Without a large national army or navy, many issues were difficult to deal with. In the 1780s, pirates took American sailors prisoner near North Africa and sold them into slavery. England maintained military posts in New York and other US territories. And Spain refused to leave frontier lands claimed by the United States. In addition, trade routes on land and sea needed to be protected if the country was to get out of debt.

7

The CONSTITUTIONAL CONVENTION

To address the nation's problems, 12 states sent 55 delegates, or representatives, to the Philadelphia State House in 1787. The Constitutional **Convention** began May 25. Delegate Edmund Randolph presented the Virginia Plan for reshaping the government. The plan included the following ideas:

- Three branches of government: legislative, executive, judicial
- A two-house legislature with one house elected by the people and one house elected by the other house
- The number of representatives for each state would be decided by state population
- An executive, chosen by the legislature, to carry out the law
- A national court system
- The executive and the national court would have the power to reject, or veto, laws
- The national government could veto state laws

It's a Fact!

Suspicious of a stronger central government, Rhode Island was the only state to refuse to send delegates to the Constitutional Convention.

George Washington was elected the president of the convention. He nearly didn't attend. Washington's presence meant people would respect the decisions of the convention.

George Washington

BORROWING FROM HISTORY

Each state had written its own constitution after declaring independence from England. Many of the ideas for the US Constitution were taken from these constitutions. The convention delegates also borrowed many ideas from the **philosophers** Baron de Montesquieu and John Locke. They used the Magna Carta, too—a British document from 1215 that made the law a higher power than the British ruler. The English Bill of Rights of 1689 inspired the US Bill of Rights.

If the Virginia Plan seems familiar, that's because it's the framework of the US Constitution. The plan's system of checks and balances promised to keep each branch of government from becoming too powerful.

However, delegates from less populated states noted that the plan meant they'd have less representation in the legislature. The New Jersey Plan suggested each state should have the same number of representatives (as they did under the Articles of Confederation). Larger states, though, felt they should have more representation because they had more people.

The Great Compromise, or Connecticut Compromise, suggested that one legislative house have equal representation (the Senate), while the other have representation according to population (the House of Representatives). The delegates agreed to this plan.

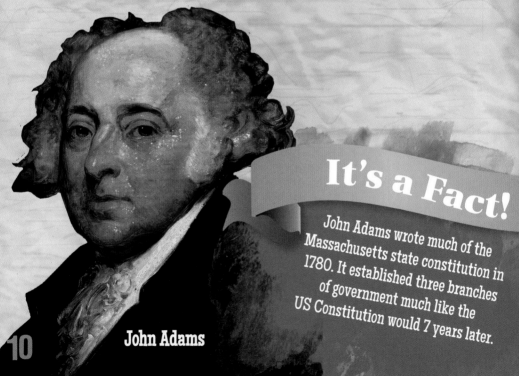

John Adams

It's a Fact!

John Adams wrote much of the Massachusetts state constitution in 1780. It established three branches of government much like the US Constitution would 7 years later.

Tensions were high during the convention. There was always the threat the delegates would leave and the convention would be a failure.

MORE COMPROMISING

Another compromise involving representation according to population brought the slavery issue into the spotlight. Should slaves be counted as part of the state population even though they weren't considered citizens? Some thought slavery should be outlawed altogether. Several compromises kept the convention from falling apart. First, a slave would be considered 3/5 of a person (every five slaves was equal to three free people). Another compromise forbade Congress from interfering in the slave trade until 1808.

11

RATIFICATION

On September 17, 1787, the US Constitution was signed by 39 of the 55 delegates. That didn't make it law yet. Nine of the 13 state governments had to approve, or ratify, it. Without one more compromise, the constitution might never have been adopted.

Opponents of the Constitution distrusted the new central, or federal, government. These "Anti-Federalists" wanted a bill of rights as protection against the expanded powers of the federal government. Supporters of the Constitution, called Federalists, argued that a list of rights was unnecessary because the Constitution only gave the government the powers listed in the document. However, the Federalists finally agreed to a bill of rights. Under the promise that the changes, called amendments, would be added, the Constitution was finally ratified in 1788.

It's a Fact!

Thomas Jefferson and John Adams weren't present at the convention. Each was serving overseas as a representative of the United States.

Federalists and Anti-Federalists tried
to persuade each state to support their view.
They became the first political parties.

Hamilton

FEDERALIST:

A COLLECTION

OF

ESSAYS,

THE FEDERALIST PAPERS

The Federalist Papers were 85 essays telling the public why the Constitution was the right choice for the United States. They were published in New York newspapers in 1787 and 1788. Each essay was signed "Publius," but there were actually several authors. We now know Alexander Hamilton (first secretary of treasury), John Jay (first chief justice of the Supreme Court), and James Madison (fourth US president) did much of the writing. However, we still don't know who wrote some of the essays.

Alexander Hamilton

John Jay

James Madison

WE the PEOPLE

The Constitution begins with an introduction called the Preamble.

We the people of the United States,

The Constitution was written on behalf of the citizens of the United States, not just a few in power.

in order to form a more perfect Union,

The Constitution was meant to fix the mistakes of the Articles of Confederation.

establish justice, insure domestic tranquility, provide for the common defense, promote the general welfare, and secure the blessings of liberty to ourselves and our posterity,

This part addresses the country's problems under the Articles and promises to work for justice, peace, and freedom.

do ordain and establish this Constitution for the United States of America.

The last section states the American people gave the Constitution power.

It's a Fact!

The Preamble focuses on why the document was created. It doesn't include any laws.

SOME KEY PLAYERS

James Madison is called the Father of the Constitution for his role in putting together the ideas in the document. He was the primary writer of the Virginia Plan as well. Gouverneur Morris is given credit for the wording of the document. "We the people" was Morris's choice for the document's beginning. The man who actually wrote the words was Jacob Shallus, who was hired for $30. The misspellings in the Constitution could be blamed on Shallus!

Gouverneur Morris

We the people of the United States, in order to form a more perfect Union, establish justice, insure domestic tranquility, provide for the common defense, promote the general welfare, and secure the blessings of liberty to ourselves and our posterity, do ordain and establish this Constitution for the United States of America.

With the adoption of the Constitution, the United States became a "union" rather than a "confederation."

The LEGISLATIVE BRANCH

The rest of the Constitution is divided into parts called articles and smaller pieces within each article called sections. Article I focuses on the legislature. It details Congress's structure, powers and limitations, and requirements to be elected. For example, House representatives must be at least 25 years old and serve 2-year terms. Senators must be at least 30 years old and serve 6-year terms.

Another section details the lawmaking process. Congressional bills are passed to the president, who may sign them into law or veto them.

The many powers of Congress mentioned in Article I include:

- to collect and set taxes;
- to make money;
- to set up post offices;
- to form and maintain an army and a navy.

It's a Fact!

In 1806, Henry Clay was appointed to the Senate though he was only 29. No one stopped him!

The Constitution allows Congress to make up its own rules about when and how to meet but states that records must be kept.

of the United States, in order to form
common defence, promote the general Welfare, and secure
this Constitution for the United States of America.

Article. I.

...n granted, shall be vested in a Congress of the United States, who

All legislative powers herein granted shall be vested in a Congress of the United States, which shall consist of a Senate and House of Representatives.

ELASTICITY AND LIMITATIONS

Section 8 of Article I gives Congress the power to make laws that aren't specifically mentioned in the Constitution. This passage, or clause, is called the **elastic** clause because it lets Congress stretch its powers "to make all laws which shall be necessary and proper" to carry out its duties. However, Section 9 says Congress cannot suspend "habeas corpus" except in times of rebellion or invasion. This means people can't be held against their will without reason.

The EXECUTIVE BRANCH

Article II created the executive branch of the government. An executive has the power to make decisions and carry them out. The Constitution gives this power to the president. It says the president must be at least 35 years old and a citizen born in the United States. It also explains the electoral college, a group that represents the voters. Among the presidential powers and duties listed are:

- to enforce laws;
- to appoint judges with approval by the Senate;
- to make treaties along with the Senate;
- to act as commander in chief of the army and navy;
- to provide Congress with information about the "state of the Union."

Concerning the president possibly abusing the power of the office, Article II instructs that the president should be removed for committing crimes.

It's a Fact!

At first, according to the Constitution, the person with the second-most number of votes was elected vice president. Now, the president and vice president are elected as a team.

Article II contains the oath, or promise, each president makes: "I do solemnly swear (or affirm) that I will faithfully execute the office of president of the United States, and will to the best of my ability, preserve, protect and defend the Constitution of the United States."

WHAT ARE CHECKS AND BALANCES?

Checks and balances written into the Constitution ensure that one branch of the government doesn't have too much power. For example, the president can veto a bill from Congress, but Congress can vote again to pass it. The House can **impeach** the president, while the Senate holds the trial. And the chief justice of the Supreme Court **presides** over the trial. Two presidents have been impeached, Andrew Johnson and Bill Clinton, but neither was proven guilty and removed from office.

The JUDICIAL BRANCH

Article III sets up the judicial branch of the government, sometimes called the judiciary. By calling it the Supreme Court, the Constitution makes this court the highest in the land. Judges serve during "good behavior," meaning for life if they don't break any laws. This protects judges from being forced from office by a president or Congress who wants a certain decision in court—another example of checks and balances. The Supreme Court may hear any case that deals with the law under the US Constitution.

This article also defines treason as declaring war against the United States or helping the nation's enemies, including "giving them aid and comfort." However, treason is an act; it's not just talking or thinking about it.

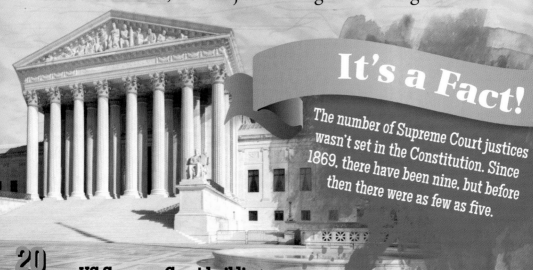

It's a Fact!

The number of Supreme Court justices wasn't set in the Constitution. Since 1869, there have been nine, but before then there were as few as five.

US Supreme Court building

In 1937, President Franklin Roosevelt tried to add six justices to the Supreme Court so that the court would accept some of his policies. However, Congress didn't agree to this.

TRIAL BY JURY

Section 2 of Article III promises citizens a trial by jury. The idea of trial by jury was an important concern to American citizens after the American Revolution. During the war, trial by jury—a right British citizens long enjoyed—had been set aside, and people had been imprisoned without trial or taken to England for trial. Later, the Bill of Rights would add that the trial had to be where the crime took place.

STATES' RIGHTS and AMENDMENTS

Article IV of the Constitution deals with issues between states. States must respect other states' laws. For example, if someone in California breaks the law, they can't go to New York for protection. The New York state government must hand over the criminal. This article also says the federal government will help the states in times of crisis.

Article V explains how the Constitution can be amended. There are two ways:

1) Two-thirds of each house of Congress can propose an amendment. Then, three-fourths of the state legislatures or state conventions must approve the amendment.

2) A constitutional convention can be called by two-thirds of the state legislatures. That meeting can propose amendments that must be ratified by three-fourths of the states.

The second method has never been used.

It's a Fact!

Article VI declares the Constitution is "the supreme law of the land." Called the supremacy clause, this means national laws top state laws.

NEW STATES

Article IV allows new states to join the nation. It says: "no new state shall be formed or erected within the **jurisdiction** of any other state" without the approval of state legislatures. However, West Virginia was created out of the western part of Virginia in 1863. The federal government allowed the new state because the rest of Virginia left the Union during the American Civil War.

irty-Eighth **Congress of the United States of America;**

At the ___Second___ Session,

and held at the City of Washington, on Monday, the ___fifth___ day of December, one thousand eight hundred and sixty=four.

A RESOLUTION

Submitting to the legislatures of the several States a proposition to amend the Constitution of the United States.

Resolved by the Senate and House of Representatives of the United States of America in Congress assembled, two-thirds of both houses concurring, that the following article be proposed to the legislatures of the several States as an amendment to the Constitution of the United States, which, when ratified by three=fourths of said Legislatures, shall be valid, to all intents and purposes, as a part of the said Constitution, namely: Article XIII. Section 1. Neither slavery nor involuntary servitude, except as a punishment for crime whereof the party shall have been duly convicted, shall exist within the United States, or any place subject to their jurisdiction. Section 2. Congress shall have power to enforce this article by appropriate legislation.

To pass an amendment today, 290 of the 435 members of the House of Representatives and 67 of the 100 senators must vote for an amendment. Thirty-eight states must approve it for it to be added to the Constitution.

Schuyler Colfax
Speaker of the House of Representatives.

H. Hamlin
Vice President of the United States and President of the Senate.

Abraham Lincoln

The BILL of RIGHTS

Congress has considered more than 9,000 amendments, but only 27 have been ratified. The first 10, called the Bill of Rights, were ratified together in 1791. These were the promised additions that paved the way for the ratification of the Constitution. The Bill of Rights includes:

First Amendment: Freedom of religion, speech, and the press; right to assemble and **petition**

Second Amendment: Right to bear arms

Third Amendment: Right to refuse housing to soldiers

Fourth Amendment: Protection against unlawful searches and seizing of property

Fifth Amendment: Rights of those accused of crimes

Sixth Amendment: Right to a fair trial

Seventh Amendment: Rights in **civil** cases

Eighth Amendment: Protection against unfair fines and "cruel and unusual punishment"

Ninth Amendment: Protection of citizens' rights not named in the Constitution

Tenth Amendment: Protection of states' rights not named in the Constitution

It's a Fact!

Despite the many rights the Constitution gives to those accused of crimes, "innocent until proven guilty" isn't one of them. It's a part of our legal system by tradition, though.

RIGHTS OF STUDENTS

The First Amendment's promise of the right to free speech often comes up in schools. Sometimes it's hard to know what rights students have. Several court cases have established rules that young people must follow. Students cannot threaten others with harm. They cannot use offensive language on school grounds or when using school materials and tools. In recent years, bullying and cyberbullying have been free-speech topics in the news.

Many of the rights given to the accused by the Constitution had been missing in the British colonies' court system in the days leading up to the American Revolution.

MORE AMENDMENTS

Seventeen more amendments followed the Bill of Rights. Here are a few:

Thirteenth Amendment: Ended slavery (1865)

Fourteenth Amendment: Made all people "born and **naturalized** in the United States" citizens (1868)

Fifteenth Amendment: Stated the right to vote "shall not be denied . . . on account of race" (1870)

Eighteenth Amendment: Prohibited the making and selling of alcohol (1919)

Nineteenth Amendment: Gave women the right to vote (1920)

Twenty-first Amendment: Repealed the Eighteenth Amendment (1933)

Twenty-second Amendment: Limited presidents to two terms of office (1951)

Twenty-fourth Amendment: Ended voting tax (1964)

Twenty-fifth Amendment: Explained order in which officials assume the presidency (1967)

Twenty-sixth Amendment: Changed the voting age to 18 (1971)

To read the full text of all amendments, see www.archives.gov or another resource about the Constitution.

It's a Fact!

When President Ronald Reagan had surgery in 1985, Vice President George H. W. Bush became president for 8 hours, thanks to the Twenty-fifth Amendment.

OUR REPUBLIC

The Seventeenth Amendment changed how senators are elected to Congress. At first, the Constitution called for them to be elected by state legislatures. However, the amendment gave that power directly to the people in 1913. You won't find the word "democracy" in the Constitution. That's because our country is actually a republic. In a democracy, we'd make the laws and decisions ourselves. Instead, we elect people to make laws and decisions for us.

The Twenty-seventh Amendment, dealing with congressional salaries, was originally proposed in 1789 but wasn't ratified until 1992!

ALWAYS AT WORK

The Constitution isn't just a piece of history. It's at work every day and affects your life in more ways than you can imagine. It's continually being tested by court cases and government decisions, too. Though the text left some ideas up to interpretation, what is clear is its success so far.

The Constitution is the oldest, single-document constitution still in effect. Just four pages of text have managed to keep our nation operating for more than 200 years. The US Constitution has inspired other nations' constitutions, including those of Japan and India. Will it be amended in the future? Probably. But the basic principles outlined in the text should allow our country to grow and change peacefully while still ensuring our rights as US citizens for years to come.

The constitution of India is the longest in the world, with more than 400 articles.

It's a Fact!

The US Constitution is the shortest constitution in the world.

THE UNITED STATES CONSTITUTION

PREAMBLE

↓

LEGISLATIVE BRANCH

↓

EXECUTIVE BRANCH

↓

JUDICIAL BRANCH

↓

STATES' ISSUES

↓

AMENDING THE CONSTITUTION

↓

THE SUPREMACY CLAUSE

↓

BILL OF RIGHTS

↓

OTHER AMENDMENTS

PRESIDENTIAL MUSICAL CHAIRS

In 1973, President Richard Nixon named Gerald Ford vice president when Vice President Spiro Agnew stepped down, or resigned. Before this, the vice-presidential position wasn't filled until the next election. In 1974, Nixon resigned, and Ford became president. Nelson Rockefeller then became vice president. The nation found itself with a president and vice president who hadn't been elected! This was all made possible by the Twenty-fifth Amendment. What might have happened in 1974 without this amendment?

GLOSSARY

civil: relating to legal actions other than criminal proceedings

constitution: the basic laws by which a country or state is governed

convention: a gathering of people who have a common interest or purpose

document: a formal piece of writing

elastic: able to go back to its shape after being stretched

impeach: to charge with misconduct in office

jurisdiction: the area over which laws can be enforced

militia: a group of citizens who organize like soldiers in order to protect themselves

naturalized: granted citizenship to somebody of foreign birth

petition: to make a written request signed by many people asking the government to take an action

philosopher: a person who tries to discover and to understand the nature of knowledge

preside: to lead or to be in a position of authority

rebellion: a fight to overthrow a government

repeal: to do away with

FOR MORE INFORMATION

BOOKS

Armentrout, David, and Patricia Armentrout. *The Constitution.* Vero Beach, FL: Rourke Publishing, 2005.

Krensky, Stephen. *The Constitution.* New York, NY: Marshall Cavendish Benchmark, 2012.

Labunski, Richard. *James Madison and the Struggle for the Bill of Rights.* New York, NY: Oxford University Press, 2006.

WEBSITES

The Constitution for Kids
www.usconstitution.net/constkids.html
Still confused about the Constitution? This easy-to-read guide has many answers.

Constitution of the United States
www.archives.gov/exhibits/charters/constitution.html
See photos of the original document and gain access to the entire text.

Constitution Resources
www.uscourts.gov/EducationalResources/ConstitutionResources.aspx
Find out more about the Constitution and the Bill of Rights on the federal courts' website.

Publisher's note to educators and parents: Our editors have carefully reviewed these websites to ensure that they are suitable for students. Many websites change frequently, however, and we cannot guarantee that a site's future contents will continue to meet our high standards of quality and educational value. Be advised that students should be closely supervised whenever they access the Internet.

INDEX